DOWN WITH WIMPS!

by Scott Corbett

illustrated by Larry Ross

E. P. Dutton   New York

Library of Congress Cataloging in Publication Data

Corbett, Scott.
  Down with wimps!

  Summary: Two mischievous girls make sure that a popular
author has an unforgettable visit to Gruberville Elementary
School.
  [1. Schools—Fiction]   I. Ross, Larry, date, ill.
II. Title.
PZ7.C79938Ds 1984   [Fic]   84-1579
ISBN 0-525-44108-5

Published in the United States by E. P. Dutton, Inc.,
2 Park Avenue, New York, N.Y. 10016

Published simultaneously in Canada by
Fitzhenry & Whiteside Limited, Toronto

Editor: Ann Durell   Designer: Isabel Warren-Lynch

Printed in the U.S.A.   COBE   First Edition
10 9 8 7 6 5 4 3 2 1

*with love
to my daughter, Florence*

ONE

•••••••••

Their principal, Mr. Kleinstein, made the announcement in Assembly himself. He liked to make the important ones.

"Two weeks from today we are going to see a Real Live Author in person! Kenneth Barr is coming here to Gruberville Elementary to talk to us!"

The cheering and squealing and clapping that greeted this announcement received no support from Claudine Boggs and Bessie Emanuelson.

"Kenneth Barr? Hey, Bessie, isn't he the one Gwen is always—"

"Sure. Look at her!"

Bessie was nearsighted and wore glasses, but she could see that Gwendolyn Willoughby was bouncing up and down in her seat like a yo-yo. Claudine groaned.

"He's the one, all right. The soupy one. Remember last year in Miss Finch's class when she read us that gloppy book?"

"Couldn't get away. Just had to sit there."

"And those drawings!"

"Saccharine tablets, every one of them. Arg!" Bessie sighed heavily. "But there's plenty of wimps like Gwen who think he's just peachy-pie wonderful."

No question about that. All you had to do was look around.

"Well, I wonder what he looks like. I'll bet he'll be four feet tall and wear one of those green hats like a leprechaun."

"Naw, he'll be an ape with a broken nose who looks like he couldn't write his own name, let alone that wimpy stuff."

"I'm curious," said Claudine. "First chance we get, let's go to the library and see."

But the first chance they got was the same one everybody else got, and by the time they walked into the library it was full of kids grabbing Kenneth Barr books while Mrs. Birdley yelled, "One apiece, now, just one apiece! Bring them to the desk and line up! I won't have all this jostling!" Even a few of the wimpier boys were among the book grabbers.

Tall, blond, willowy Gwendolyn—Willowy Willoughby, Claudine called her—was right in the thick of things. When they came in, she was yanking *Chin Up, Jamie!* out of Fran Vinney's hands.

"But I saw it first!" said Fran.

"You grabbed it first! I saw it first!"

Claudine wondered how you could prove that. Short, squat, and chunky, she glared up at Gwen from under dark, squared-off bangs.

"Aw, for Pete's sake, Gwen, let her have it! You must have read it ten times already!"

"Twelve," said Gwen, gazing down at her from cool blond heights, "and every time it gets better. And who asked you, anyway? I suppose *you* want it, too?"

"Like a bad cold."

Gwen laughed smugly. First she looked down at Claudine, then up at Bessie, because Bessie was even taller than she, and blond, too. The big difference was, Bessie wore glasses and had a figure like a lead pencil.

"Sour grapes," sneered Gwen. "You always pretend you don't like Kenneth Barr books, but you know you do. *Everyone* does."

"I've had hangnails I liked better," said Bessie, "but let's see his picture. We were wondering what he looks like."

Gwen got off one of her silvery laughs. She waved a pitying hand at Claudine and Bessie.

"Think of it! They don't even know his picture *never* appears on his books!"

Several copies were thrust under their noses, and book jackets were flipped to show them. It was true. No photo of the author.

"What's the matter with him?" asked Claudine.

"Can't decide which head to show," suggested Bessie.

"Oh, shut up, Goggle-Eyes," suggested Gwen. "You don't think he'd go around visiting schools if he wasn't good-looking. It's just part of his—well, his mystery. In fact, I'd bet *anything* he's very good-looking!"

"Fifty cents," said Claudine.

"You're on!" Gwen's blue eyes were suddenly small and glittery. She sent a smirking glance around at the other Barr fans, then poured it on Claudine. "Don't forget your money the day he comes!"

"You got carried away," said Bessie when they were alone again. "That's fifty cents down the drain."

"Why? Remember that author who came two years ago? She looked like a gargoyle, but that didn't stop her from showing up."

"Sure, sure—but I don't trust sneaky Gwen. I've got a hunch she's onto something. She was so sure of herself. Remember what a tightwad she is. She'd only bet on a sure thing."

Claudine was beginning to have an uneasy feeling herself, but of course she tried to brave it out.

"Well, I'm not worried. Remember, she said gorgeous. Not just good-looking. Gorgeous."

"The bet was 'very good-looking,'" Bessie reminded her, "and I'm worried. That Gwen . . ."

Naturally Gruberville Elementary went to work on a big welcome for its Real Live Author. Signs were lettered. There was a poster contest, won as usual by Rinky Berman. His poster copied an illustration from *Jamie Gets the Jimjams,* which looked quite a bit like the original if you stood across the room from it. All the other posters went up, too, to give the halls a festive air. The PTA planned a reception for Mr. Barr in the library after his talk. All the teachers read one of his books to their classes, including Claudine and Bessie's teacher, though the expression that sometimes flitted across Mrs. Hindle's face while she was reading made them feel pretty sure she was not big on Barr. And of course every Barr book in the library was kept circulating right up to the time he was scheduled to show up.

The great day came. Bells rang for Assembly. The famous author had phoned from his motel and was due any minute. Gwendolyn Willoughby and the other special Kenneth Barr fans had been chosen as a welcoming committee to escort him to the gymnasium. They were waiting by the front doors with special sashes across their fronts, squirming and giggling with excitement. Mr. Kleinstein was fidgeting on the platform that was installed whenever the gymnasium became the auditorium. The lower grades were filing in and filling up the front rows. Claudine and Bessie were sitting on the aisle with their class, just in front of Mrs. Hindle, when she said the words that started everything.

"Oh, drat, I forgot the tape recorder, and Mr. Kleinstein told me to plug it in by the stage and record Mr. Barr's talk!"

Claudine and Bessie's heads swiveled around.

"We'll get it!"

"Know just where it is!"

They were on their feet and out of the room before anyone else could think of stirring. Mrs. Hindle let them go, too. She knew that when something practical needed to be done, they could be counted on to get moving and do it. Mr. K. did not miss their exit, however, and his startled frown showed how little he liked the idea of their being out of his sight for a moment at such a crucial time.

They rushed down the halls and around to their classroom, and they were just picking up the cassette tape recorder when the classroom door was flung open and a man rushed in shouting in a whisper,

"Hide me!"

TWO
• • • • • • • • • • • •

He swung the door closed and crouched behind
it, while Claudine and Bessie stared at him with their
jaws flapping in the breeze. After a few seconds,
through the window in the door, they could see Miss
Trisket, the school nurse, walk past out in the hall.
The man stared up at them and spoke in a hoarse
voice.

"Has she gone?"

"Miss Trisket?"

"Yes! Sheila Trisket?"

"That's right. She's our school nurse."

The man groaned.

"I knew it! I just caught a glimpse of her, but I
was sure. . . . Good grief, what'll I do?"

Now that she'd had a good look at the stranger,
Claudine wanted to groan, too. She saw fifty cents

going down the drain. Here was this medium-tall, not especially dark but wildly handsome stranger—handsome in a sort of thin, nervous way, and . . .

"Say, are you Kenneth Barr?"

He nodded miserably.

"Yes. And just a few years ago, I was everything to Sheila Trisket. But then one night I left town, moving on, and— Why, when she sees me, I don't know what she'll do, but she'll make a terrible scene! Of all the rotten luck!"

"Funny, she hasn't said anything about knowing you that well."

"Oh, but Kenneth Barr's not my real name. And I knew her before I started writing my books."

"Oh. Well—and your picture isn't up anywhere, because you don't have it on your books."

"Wouldn't dare." A faintly self-satisfied smirk slipped across his face and quickly disappeared. "She's just one of many, I'm afraid. All through my teens and twenties, I was a pretty awful heartbreaker—and now I'm paying for it. This country is full of women who have never gotten over me and would like to kill me on sight, if they could. I've always been afraid I might run into one of them again—and now it's happened. When I walk into your auditorium . . ."

"But Miss Trisket won't be there," said Bessie. "She never comes to Assembly. And besides— Ow!"

Bessie said "Ow!" because Claudine had stepped on her toe. She got the message.

"Sorry, Bessie. Besides, I heard her say authors bore her."

9

"Oh, did she?" said Kenneth Barr, frowning a little at that. "That would be just like her." But then he brightened up. "So you think she'll stay put while I'm here?"

"You can bet on it," said Claudine. "But—what are you doing back here, anyway?"

"I guess I came in the wrong door."

"You sure did. You better go out and scoot around the building and come in the front, where the big welcoming committee's waiting."

"And you won't have to walk past Trisket's office that way," said Bessie.

"Just show me where to go!"

They gave him directions. After a furtive look up and down the corridor, he took off. Bessie sighed.

"Well, I didn't want to worry you, but I did hear a rumor."

"What rumor?"

"I heard Gwen knew he was good-looking. Some cousin of hers told her."

Claudine sighed for her fifty cents, but said, "Never mind. We've got something else to think about. Come on, I'll tell you on the way back. . . ."

"Great idea!" agreed Bessie, when Claudine had told her. "I wouldn't miss it! But why don't you do it yourself?"

"Well, there was that time in the third grade—"

"One time!"

"Yes, but I know you can do it."

"Oh, all right."

10

Mrs. Hindle met them at the door of the auditorium, which was buzzing with conversation as everyone waited.

"Did you have trouble—"

"No, it's okay, Mrs. Hindle. Here's everything you need."

Mrs. Hindle mouthed words at Mr. Kleinstein, who looked relieved. He, in turn, mouthed words at Claudine and Bessie as he pointed a stern finger at two unoccupied seats in the front row.

"Sit there!" were the words he mouthed, and he might as well have added, "where I can keep an eye on you!" The girls glanced at each other with pleased surprise.

"Perfect!"

"Couldn't be better!"

A clatter of footsteps and a lot of twittering and giggling in the hall made it clear that Kenneth Barr had found his way around the building and was being escorted in by Gwen & Company. The double doors were swept open, and he entered and made a little run up the steps onto the platform just like one of those people who win Oscars or Emmies on television. And on her way back to her seat, Gwen smiled sweetly at Claudine.

"You owe me fifty cents."

"You'll get it."

Everyone applauded while Kenneth Barr shook hands with Mr. Kleinstein and then beamed at the

11

audience. He sat down while Mr. K. introduced the PTA president, Mrs. Biedermeier, who introduced the speaker.

You had to admit he was good. He talked about his books, did some drawings on a big scratch pad that had been mounted on an easel for him, and gave everybody a good time, boys and girls alike. But Claudine and Bessie began to tense up, because time was running out and it was plain that before long he would be finished. Finally Claudine took a deep breath and whispered, "You're on."

"Okay, here goes."

Bessie stood up and groaned and toppled over like a tall pine in front of everybody.

"I'll get the nurse!" cried Claudine.

Kenneth Barr was goggling at them and waving his arms.

"No! Wait! I can take care of her! I—I—I've had paramedic training—!"

But Claudine was gone. Short and squat she might be, but when she moved, she moved. Kenneth Barr rushed down from the stage, looking as if he'd like to keep right on rushing out the door but didn't dare, and he was bending over Bessie, who was fluttering her eyelids now and saying, "Where am I?" when Trisket came hurrying in, followed closely by Claudine. Kenneth Barr looked up as if he expected Trisket to be waving a sword. She stared at him for an instant, then laughed heartily.

"Harold Dingle!" she cried. "What are you doing here?"

He gulped.

"Er—I'm Kenneth Barr, Sheila."

"What? You wrote those books?" This time she giggled. "Oh, I might have known you'd come to a bad end. You were always such a silly boy."

Kenneth Barr looked absolutely stunned.

"Sheila! You mean—you're not mad at me?"

"Mad? Why should I be mad? Puppy love, that's all it was with us, Harold. Oh, when you took off I had a good sniffle, but not even a good cry, really, and two days later I was dating Wilcox Butts—remember Wilcox?"

"Wilcox Butts?" Kenneth Barr staggered to his feet. "I can't believe it!"

"Well, it didn't last long—but never mind all that, look at this!" Miss Trisket proudly thrust forward her left hand, upon which sparkled a modest diamond solitaire. "I'm engaged! He's the most wonderful guy—you've got to meet him!"

"Yes, sure, I'll look forward to— Listen, I guess I'd better get back up there and— Wait a minute!" Suddenly Kenneth Barr remembered Bessie, who was sitting up now and not missing a word. He pointed a quivering finger down at her. "What—what—?"

"Oh, I'm fine now," said Bessie, getting up briskly. "It was just . . . temporary—"

"You come with me to my office," ordered Trisket with a glint in her eye. "I want to make sure you're all right."

"I'll help her," said Claudine, grabbing Bessie's arm as if she were an invalid.

13

"I'll be along in a minute," said Kenneth Barr. "I want to have a word with these two."

"And I want Miss Trisket to bring you to my office after that!" Mr. K. thundered at the girls.

Back in her office, Trisket took a long look at the two of them and collapsed into a chair, whooping. When she recovered, they talked it all over, and they were ready for Kenneth Barr when he stormed in. He pointed one hand at them and the other at Trisket.

"Why didn't you tell me she was engaged?"

"Because you were talking so silly," said Claudine.

"You needed a kick in the pants," said Bessie.

"I never heard of anything sillier, Harold," said Trisket. "Stop worrying about all those broken hearts—they don't stay broken, believe me!"

"Life goes on," said Bessie.

"You ought to see her boyfriend. He's an All-American hunk!"

"Thank you, Claudine," said Miss Trisket primly. "Now, don't take it so hard, Harold," she added, for by now he was sitting in a chair with his head in his hands. But when he looked up, he began to perk up.

"You mean, I'm a free man? I can put my picture on my jackets now? Boy! My publishers will dance with joy!"

"Now you're talking!" said Claudine.

The meeting in Mr. K's office was something else again. Simba, they called him at school—*Simba* was African for "lion"—because of his heavy mane of tawny hair. He was also known as Redfang because

of his large, ferocious teeth, and that day he lived up to both nicknames.

"I want to get to the bottom of this!" he roared. "I'm going to make an example of these girls! The idea! Disrupting a special event, putting on a phony fainting spell—"

"Oh, I'm not sure I could safely diagnose it as phony, Mr. Kleinstein," said Trisket with a straight face.

Simba pulled his head back like a baffled King of the Beasts, shook his bristling mane and turned to their visitor.

"Well, surely, Mr. Barr, you must feel you suffered undue humiliation and—"

But Mr. Barr shook his head.

"Oh, no, not at all. I have no complaints against them at all; in fact, I think they behaved very well."

Mr. Kleinstein scrunched down in his chair, getting redder and redder. He knew there was something he didn't know, but he didn't know how to get at it. Finally he jabbed an imperial finger in the direction of Claudine and Bessie.

"Out! Out! And don't let me even catch sight of you two for at least three days!"

It was a small price to pay.

THREE
●●●●●●●●●●●●●

Of course, Gwen Willoughby was livid with rage.
Like everyone else in their class, she soon knew they
had not only been to Trisket's office but to Mr.
Kleinstein's, along with Trisket and Kenneth Barr,
but nobody could seem to get a line on what really
happened. The worst of it was, Claudine and Bessie
weren't even thrown out of school! They came back
to class acting as if nothing had happened, and all
they would say was, "Everything's fine."

When school was over and Mrs. Hindle dismissed
their class, Claudine had her fifty cents ready when
Gwen came her way. But Gwen was so desperate, she
even tried to be friendly. Instead of taking the
money, she pulled Claudine to one side.

"Listen, Claudine, just tell me what went on in

the Lion's Den"—what everybody called Mr. K's office—"and I won't tell another soul and I'll forget our bet. You can *keep* the money!"

"Nothing happened," said Claudine. "Everything was fine."

Gwen stared at her with horror and loathing. She couldn't believe anybody would pass up a chance to keep money.

"You're a liar!" She snatched the fifty cents out of Claudine's hand and marched away, a ramrod of righteous indignation. Claudine glanced at Bessie.

"It was worth every cent."

"I was almost tempted to go halvers with you," said Bessie.

Claudine watched Gwen disappear down the hall and thought how wonderful it would be to have Willowy Willoughby's blossoming figure without her mean mind.

"It's funny, when you know her folks are almost the richest people in town."

"Well, one thing is sure," said Bessie. "She's our sworn enemy."

"She sure is. Especially mine."

To tell the truth, Gwendolyn Willoughby wasn't the only person Claudine and Bessie weren't popular with. They made about half of their class uncomfortable, and that included some of the boys like stuffy Roddy Plover. They were always coming up with crazy deadpan remarks and doing things you wished you had the nerve to do but didn't. They didn't just go along with whatever happened, the easy way. That scheming mind of Claudine's seemed to *cause* things to happen.

But there were others in the class who thought they were okay, so it wasn't all bad. The teachers? Well . . . they were divided. Last year, with Miss Finch, things had been tough. This year, with Mrs. Hindle, they had someone who could put up with them.

They started down the hall, but then Bessie found she had forgotten a notebook, so they had to go back for the notebook, and then Bessie couldn't find her glasses case, so they had to go back and look for her glasses case. Bessie was a great forgetter. While they were looking, the case fell out of the notebook— "Now, how did it get in there?" marveled Bessie— and they made a third try at leaving. By then, the halls were empty.

"Come on, Bessie, move! If we don't watch it, we'll miss our bus. . . . Okay, tiptoes, everybody," Claudine added as they approached the danger area, where corridors crossed and ahead up the hall was the Cage—as the Lion's Den was also called.

"Maybe we ought to go around, Claudine."

"No time for that, and anyway, he's probably left by now."

At that instant, the door to the Cage opened. A tall, slim, blond young woman with a cool, crisp, no-nonsense look about her stepped into the hall, with the sound of a familiar voice right behind her. Claudine and Bessie did a snappy slide-turn any drum majorette would have envied and shot down the hall to the right. "Don't let me catch sight of you for at least three days!" he'd said, and here it was only hours later and they were obviously late for their bus!

"In here, Bessie! We'll cut through the cafeteria!"

They were out of sight, but not out of range of Redfang's foghorn voice. They could hear him coming their way, saying,

"I think you'll find our cafeteria to be as well-equipped as any in the state school system!"

"I'm eager to see it," said the visitor. "It's hard for a dietitian to be totally effective with outmoded equipment—we learned that at Cornell."

"They're coming here!" groaned Bessie. The girls rushed across the empty, silent cafeteria and flung themselves against the far doors.

Locked!

Claudine stared around wildly, and pointed. They dived under a table just before Simba and his visitor walked in. It isn't easy diving under a table when your arms are full of books. It was a good thing there had been refreshments for Kenneth Barr and the PTA mothers after his talk, or there wouldn't have been a tablecloth hanging down from the table to hide them.

"Well, here we are, Miss Forbush. I'm afraid the place is not at its best after the reception for Mr. Barr, but— Look at this, now! Cookie plates and a cloth left on this table!" snapped Mr. K. They gave up breathing as the tablecloth twitched under his impatient fingers. "I've a good mind to take this to my office and confront Mrs. Bunny with it tomorrow morning! *Everything* should have been tidied up before she left!"

"It will be from now on," said Miss Forbush in a cool, firm voice. "The importance of neatness was drummed into us dietitians at Cornell."

"I'm sure it was," said Mr. K., while Claudine with her eyes screwed shut waited for the tablecloth to be whisked away and for the human volcano to erupt. What on earth could they say? "We were just looking for a quiet place to study"?

"Well, it's too late to teach the woman anything—she's leaving, anyway," he decided, and took his hand off the tablecloth.

He led Miss Forbush around the counter and into the kitchen, foghorning away about everything as they went. The minute they knew he was safely in the kitchen, Claudine whispered, "Now! And don't *bump* anything!"

Because of their armload of books, they had to walk out from under the table on their knees. Still, all might have been well if Bessie had gotten her head all the way out from under the tablecloth before she stood up. But she didn't. When she straightened up, she was wearing the cloth, and cookie plates were crashing onto the floor. A startled roar from the kitchen shook the walls.

"What was that?"

Bessie twisted loose from the tablecloth, and they made a tiptoe rush for the door to the hall. Fortunately Mr. K. had left it half-open. They were on their way down the hall before he even got out of the kitchen. Nobody was in sight anywhere. They zipped down the corridor and out a side door undetected.

"Hurry, we can still make the bus!" said Bessie, and started toward the front of the building. Claudine nearly yanked her arm out of its socket stopping her.

"Are you crazy? And let Redfang see us running away? Come on!" Claudine dragged her in the other direction, toward some friendly shrubbery where they could hide. That put them under the cafeteria windows and let them hear Mr. K. saying, "Now, what on earth made that fool cloth slip off the table?" That made them feel better. Hot pursuit was not a danger, after all.

"Okay, let's go!" said Claudine. They ran around the side of the building to the front just in time to see their schoolbus disappearing down the drive. Mr. Feeney waited just so long, and he didn't come running in looking for you. He went. The kids on Mr. Feeney's bus got home on time, no matter who was missing. The girls sighed. For them, there was none

of this stuff of phoning home and whining, "Mummy, I missed my bus, will you come and get me?" They both had working mothers.

"Well, it's a nice day," said Bessie, "so I think I'll walk."

"I think you will, too," said Claudine, and they did.

FOUR
●●●●●●●●●●●●●

It was a long walk home, and not an easy one for Claudine. Her short legs were no match for Bessie's long ones. She kept having to say, "Slow down, will you? Honest, Bessie, walking with you is like walking with a stork!" And Bessie did look like a tall, solemn bird, when you thought about it.

They had plenty of time to talk. After hashing over everything else, they got back to Miss Forbush.

"I guess she's going to be our new cook, all right."

"Dietitian," said Claudine. "You heard all that talk about the training she had in college. Cornell. She must have said it fifteen times. That must be a special college for cooking, the way she talked. But anyway, almost anything will beat Mrs. Bunny's food."

Mrs. Bunny was a nice, motherly woman, but the stuff she shoveled out to them in the cafeteria was generally rated somewhere between "bleh!" and "ugh!" Bunny Sludge, they called it. When the notice announcing her retirement went around, teachers closed their classroom doors so that Mrs. Bunny wouldn't hear the cheers.

"We've got nowhere to go but up," said Claudine, but Bessie took her usual view of things.

"Well, I don't know. No matter how bad food is, it can always get worse."

"Oh, Bessie, knock it off!" snapped Claudine. It annoyed her to have Bessie talk like that, especially since she was so often right.

When they finally got to Claudine's house, her father was in his little study on the first floor wearing his usual distracted look, tee shirt, and rumpled slacks. He was a physics teacher at the high school, and a computer nut on the side—or maybe the other way around. When they walked in, he appeared to be correcting papers, but Claudine knew from his shifty eyes that he'd been fooling around with the computer he'd built himself.

"Hi, girls. What's new?"

Claudine decided to leave out a few details for the time being.

"We're going to have a new cook named Miss Forbush who's a dietitian from Cornell."

"Cornell, eh?" A crooked grin twisted her father's face sideways. "Wait'll your mother hears that."

"What do you mean?"

"It's her story, and she'll be home soon." Mr. Boggs left them dangling.

Claudine's mother was a social worker at the county office. When she showed up a few minutes later, they hardly let her get a foot in the door before telling her about Miss Forbush and demanding to know what was so funny about Cornell. She glanced at her husband, who raised his hands and grinned.

"I told them it's your story, Carol."

She looked around at them all, and shuddered.

"A dietitian from Cornell University? Well, if she's anything like *my* roommate when I was working in Chicago, after I got out of college, I feel sorry for you. There were four of us, including this Cornell-graduate dietitian; four of us living in total squalor on nothing a week. We all took turns cooking. She was the only trained cook among us, and we *dreaded* when her night came around. She had no sense of taste, of what tasted good. Her cooking was all theory."

Claudine groaned, and stared resentfully at Bessie. Was she going to be right again? Were they in for something even worse than Bunny Sludge?

And of course her father had to be his usual witty self.

"Look at the bright side, Claudine. Here's your chance to diet!"

Miss Forbush's reign began on Monday. When Claudine heard what was on the menu, she lost no time bringing the gagging news to Bessie.

"What's the champion worst thing we ever get?"

"That's a tough one. Let me think. . . ."

"How about Spanish rice?"

"That's it!"

"And that's what we're getting."

As it happened, their class was the first to go through the line that morning—"Everything bad happens to us!" mourned Bessie. The servers were at their places: Mrs. Frimstead at the Spanish rice, Mrs. Kluttz at the salad. And standing behind them, looking slim, trim, and efficient, was Miss Forbush, keeping an eye on everything.

One of Bessie's bad habits—at least, her teachers didn't think much of it—was a tendency to stick a pencil behind her ear. She found it a very convenient place to carry a pencil. She had a long one behind her ear that morning. And when she bent forward in her nearsighted way to see if the Spanish rice looked as revolting as she thought it would, the pencil shot down into the pan like a spear. Bessie gasped, and began to paw around in the rice to get it back.

"Please! Take your hand out of that rice!"

Miss Forbush had swooped forward between the servers and brushed Bessie's hand smartly aside. Her move sent the pencil and a considerable glob of rice flying into the salad bowl. Mrs. Kluttz, whom nothing bothered, stolidly fork-and-spooned the pencil out onto Bessie's plate along with a helping of salad; Mrs. Frimstead added Spanish rice; and Bessie rushed away to a table in a corner. Behind her, down the line, Gwendolyn's silvery laughter managed to reach

her through all the other giggling. When Claudine joined her, Bessie's normally pale face was still red.

"Bessie, I *knew* that pencil would get you in trouble someday!"

"I don't understand it! I must have loose ears today! Even with my glasses on, I've never had a pencil slip before!"

"Yes, you have, but not into food!" Claudine glared at her plate, pushed her salad around, and drummed fingers on the table. "We've got to organize. Stage a protest. We ... What are you doing?"

Bessie was digging her fork into the glop.

"Listen, she's got her eye on me. Maybe she won't report me if I eat this stuff and pretend to like it. I've got to!"

Bessie took a big bite. She chewed, swallowed, and her face lit up. Claudine watched admiringly.

"Say, you ought to be an actress. What a performance! The way you look, anyone would think that gook was delicious!"

Bessie stared at her with wide-eyed wonder.

"It is!"

Flabbergasted, Claudine watched Bessie gobble for a moment, then tried a dainty bite herself. Her eyes opened wide, closed blissfully, and opened wide again.

"Bessie! You're not kidding!"

There was Spanish rice, it seemed, and then there was Spanish rice *à la Forbush,* and Spanish rice *à la*

Forbush was *good!* She looked at the salad curiously, tried it, and exclaimed,

"Listen, this salad is good, too!"

Bessie was astonished. Usually Claudine wasn't big on anything that wasn't fattening. She tasted the salad herself.

"It's gorgeous!"

By then, other classes were coming through the line and filling up the tables, and all around them they could hear excited comments. Then the third grade showed up. Claudine's brother, Ferdy, and Gwendolyn's brother, Quentin, were in the third grade, and Quentin was already a living legend. He was the worst little stinker in the history of Gruberville Elementary, and that took in some tough competition.

"There's Quentin," said Claudine. "This ought to be good."

"It's a shame to waste food like this on *him!*"

Quentin Willoughby was a pudgy kid with a chubby face and a fat lower lip that stuck out in a permanent pout, over which was lowered an almost permanent frown. The pout was all there as he stared down at the Spanish rice.

"Yuk!" said Quentin.

Mrs. Frimstead gave him a small helping and a sharp look and snapped, "Move along, Quentin!"

"You can't make me eat it!"

By then, Mrs. Kluttz had installed his salad and jerked her head at him. Quentin went his sullen way.

31

They watched him plod to a table and then go through the same experience they'd had. Quentin wasn't the kind who would admit the food was wonderful, but they noticed he didn't leave anything on his plate.

"Well, I never said all Cornell-trained dietitians were terrible cooks. Just the one I knew," said Mrs. Boggs when she heard the news. "If your Miss Forbush had been my roommate, I'd have a completely different attitude today!"

Tuesday's menu sounded like a challenge almost equal to Spanish rice. Macaroni and cheese. In Mrs. Bunny's hands, macaroni and cheese had been something right out of the library paste jar. Yet once again, Miss Forbush triumphed. When she had finished hers, Claudine sat back in a swoon of pleasure.

"Cordon blew," she said, or anyway Bessie thought so.

"Blew what?" she asked.

"Cordon *blur,* you dummy!" said Claudine, that being as close as she could come to *cordon bleu.* "That's French for 'blue ribbon!' "

"I didn't know macaroni and cheese was French," said Bessie, and Claudine gave up.

Sensational hamburgers followed on Wednesday, and then came Thursday, a day none of them would ever forget, because Thursday was the first day they had Forbush's pizza. Claudine and Bessie were sitting at a table with Eddie Russo and Fran Vinney and Rinky Berman, and everybody was ecstatic except Gwendolyn Willoughby, at the next table, who wasn't feeling well and was being very dramatic about it. Even so, Gwen managed to eat her slice.

"I can't believe this!" said Eddie Russo. "Forbush doesn't *look* Italian, so how can she make the best pizza I ever tasted? We ought to give her a standing O!"

No sooner said than done—they sprang to their feet and gave Forbush a standing ovation. Her cheeks turned a nice shade of pink, and she managed a little smile and a little bow that made them whoop. Actually, she had already begun to look much more relaxed as she stood at her place at lunchtime. She was still cool and crisp, but with a bit less starch and stiffness about her each day.

The next morning, Gwendolyn Willoughby was not in school. Somebody said she'd broken out in spots and blamed it on something she was allergic to in Forbush's pizza. She missed Friday's fish and chips, which were divine.

"Eddie was right," said Claudine. "I just can't believe this!"

"Neither can I," said Bessie mournfully. "Too good to last."

Claudine glared at her.

"Now, cut it out! Bessie, if you put the whammy on this, I'll never forgive you!"

"Well, I said the food could always get worse, and

it didn't, so I was wrong about that. Maybe I'll be wrong about this," said Bessie, and sighed. "But I doubt it."

Another glorious week went by in the Gourmet Room, as they now called the cafeteria, and then one night Claudine's mother came home from a PTA meeting. When she heard her parents talking in the kitchen, Claudine went downstairs. She was hoping to wangle permission to open the refrigerator and look around; stern efforts were being made at home to starve a few pounds off her just then.

Her mother was reporting on the meeting.

"Gladys Willoughby was in full cry again. This time it's nutrition. That cookbook has really gone to her head."

"What cookbook?"

"I *told* you about it, George. You never listen! One of the national organizations has put out a cookbook called *The No-Junk-Food Cookbook,* and she has a recipe in it, so now she's the local authority on nutrition."

"That, too? Honestly, that woman—"

"She kept waving her cookbook at us and saying it pointed the way to a sensible school diet for our children—all her cracks being aimed at the new dietitian, of course, whom she finds very disappointing in this respect."

Claudine was outraged. She rushed to the attack.

"She's got a nerve! I'll bet she's only doing it because Gwen thinks she's allergic to Forbush's pizza!"

Claudine's tiny kid brother Ferdy, who had turned up to complete the family circle, put his little shoulder to the wheel, too.

"They better not pick on Forbush! Even Rottenquentin doesn't gripe anymore!"

In the third grade, "Rotten Quentin" was all one word.

"Well, I hate to say so, but she had some backing," said Mrs. Boggs. "Some of the mothers are tired of hearing about how good the food is at school—their kids are getting picky at home."

"They oughta! Some got mothers can even louse up TV dinners!" said Ferdy, who sometimes spoke in a shorthand all his own. Claudine looked at him admiringly.

"You know something, Ferdy, you can really turn a phrase," she said. "He's right, Mom—they're just jealous!"

"Maybe so, but—"

"A Committee Is Being Formed," said Mr. Boggs in a voice of doom.

"Darling, how did you know?" asked Mrs. Boggs. "That's right. A committee was formed to consult sources such as *The No-Junk-Food Cookbook* and come up with some recommendations for improved school menus."

"Then there's nothing to worry about, kids," said their father. "If it's like most committees, they'll talk and talk and nothing will be done."

"I'm not so sure, George," said their mother. "Needless to say, Gladys Willoughby is heading up the committee."

Claudine groaned. She wasn't so sure, either. She kept remembering what Bessie had said:

"Too good to last."

FIVE

Claudine told Bessie the bad news on the bus next morning. Bessie's long face grew longer, and she heaved one of her mournful sighs.

"Well, like I said— Ouch!" said Bessie, because Claudine had pinched her.

"Don't say it! I don't want to hear it! There's got to be some way to keep that committee from lousing things up!"

"I hope you can think of one."

"I'm working on it," said Claudine grimly, and she was still working on it as they trudged up the hall and came to Trisket's office. The door was open. Trisket waved to them.

"Hi, girls. How are you feeling these days, Bessie?"

Trisket! She was a good one to talk to. Claudine slid to a stop and all but butted Bessie into the nurse's office.

"Bessie's having a relapse."

"I'm what?" cried Bessie.

"We've got to talk to you. Can I close the door? We've got something private to discuss."

"Sure, Claudine, shut the door. What is it? Have you thought of a new question to ask about sex?"

"No, this is serious! It's about For—Miss Forbush. Have you heard about the PTA meeting last night?"

Trisket stopped joking. She frowned and ran a hand through her short, glossy black hair.

"I sure have!"

She reached up, took down a book, and glared at it.

"What's that?" asked Bessie.

"The No-Junk-Food Cookbook. I *knew* this would be trouble the minute I saw it, the minute Mrs. Willoughby started passing out copies of it to everyone connected with the health and welfare of this school. She gave me a copy along with some pointed remarks about how many schools—'the more progressive schools'—were using it."

She slammed the book down on the desk.

"Do you know what's going to happen if those women start throwing recipes at Inga Forbush and telling her to use them? She's a great cook, and all great cooks are temperamental. She'll throw them right back and quit!"

"Quit?" cried Bessie. "That would be awful!"

"I can't believe it!" cried Claudine. "Temperamental? Why, she looks as cool as a cucumber all the time! You should have heard her talk to Simba when—"

"What's this? When did you hear her talking to him?" asked Trisket, and then of course all of that had to come out. When they had told her all about what went on in the cafeteria, and she had dried her eyes on a piece of tissue, Trisket said,

"Well, don't you kid yourself. She can put up a great front, but when she first came here, she was scared to death—she's told me so. And she's really pleased with the way the kids like her food, but— Well, she's no namby-pamby, that's for sure, and if someone like Mrs. Willoughby starts trying to give orders, we can kiss her pizza good-bye. And to think of it, I know the Willoughbys have a cook, so I'll bet you Her Highness *never* cooks anything herself. With her, it's all theory. She talks a big game."

"Like my mom's roommate!" said Claudine. "Can I look at that book?"

"Sure, have a look. Now, I'm not saying those recipes are bad, but—"

"Where's Mrs. Willoughby's?"

"Look in the index under Broccoli Surprise."

Claudine almost dropped the book.

39

"Broccoli *Surprise?*"

"How can broccoli surprise anyone?" marveled Bessie. "Everybody already knows how awful it is!"

"Now, be fair," said Trisket, trying to be fair herself. "Broccoli is full of vitamins and other goodies, and lots of kids like it."

"Name one."

"Don't press me."

Claudine slid down in her chair with a dreamy, faraway look on her face that Bessie instantly recognized.

"Claudine," she said, with hope quivering in her voice, "have you got an idea?"

"Karate," said Claudine. "Beat 'em to the punch. Miss Trisket, has Forbush got any sense of humor?"

"Believe it or not, yes. Why? Claudine, what are you babbling about?"

Claudine told them.

That was Friday. Monday morning, classes were humming along nicely, with everyone looking forward to lunch, because Forbush had scheduled Monday as another pizza day.

But just before lunchtime, a note from Miss Forbush was circulated to all the teachers. Claudine and Bessie watched Mrs. Hindle's face fall as she read hers. She didn't read it aloud, but they knew what it said.

To all teachers: In order to comply with what we know to be the wishes of our Parent-Teacher Association, I have worked all weekend to prepare a new set of menus for this week, taken from *The No-Junk-Food Cookbook* published by the National Association of Parent-Teacher Associations Concerned with Nutrition. We hope all of you will cooperate to make this week a real nutritional breakthrough for Gruberville Elementary!

Inga Forbush
Dietitian

P.S.—Please do not announce the change to your class until you reach your tables, since we need to observe spontaneous reactions to the new menus as a guide to possible changes and adjustments as we go along.

Mrs. Hindle seemed to take a deep breath and brace herself before ordering them to get ready for the march to the cafeteria.

When they hit the line there, nobody could believe it.

"Where's the pizza?"

"I've been waiting all morning!"

"What's *this* stuff?"

Standing in her usual place, Miss Forbush looked as cool and crisp as ever, if you allowed for slightly heightened color in her cheeks.

"Your teacher will explain the change when you have gone to your tables," she said. "Please give it a try."

"Well, what is it?" someone asked.

"Broccoli Surprise," said Miss Forbush.

A general groan went up from everyone but Gwendolyn Willoughby. For an instant Gwen swayed like a willow, but then she pulled herself together and said,

"Well, *I* think it looks delicious, and I think we should all cooperate!"

So some took their helping of Broccoli Surprise because Gwen had spoken, and the rest took it because they couldn't believe Miss Forbush could really serve anything too awful.

They were wrong. It wasn't that Broccoli Surprise was nauseating—it was simply boring beyond belief. But at least Forbush had served some delicious noodles with it, and after a couple of tastes of the Surprise—everyone agreed it was *that,* all right—they made do with their noodles. All but Gwen and a few of her followers, who went all the way. Claudine had seldom enjoyed anything more than watching Gwen try to choke down her Broccoli Surprise.

At the same time, other classes had come through the line, and other classes were putting up with their surprise lunch without making any real fuss.

"This could be disaster," moaned Bessie. "There's got to be a real protest, or we're dead!"

"If you keep talking like that, you'll be dead, all right, because I'll kill you. Darn it, what's holding the third grade, anyway?"

Finally the third grade showed up.

"Ferdy's going to love this," said Claudine. But Ferdy, though he registered disappointment, took his portion and slumped away to a table, a Forbush supporter to the end.

Then came Quentin Willoughby, who obviously had been talking in line as usual instead of paying attention, and hadn't noticed anything yet. Mrs. Frimstead slid a plate onto his tray. Quentin stared down at it.

"Hey, what's *this?* Where's my pizza?"

"It's Broccoli Surprise, Quentin, now move along," said Mrs. Frimstead sharply.

Quentin's eyes popped.

"Broccoli Surprise? *Guggggg!*" screamed Quentin in a purple passion, and threw his tray straight up in the air.

"Mummy never makes us eat it. I won't eat it here!"

For once in his life, Quentin was popular. A roar of approval went up all over the cafeteria, and a lot of other Broccoli Surprises got dumped on tables in the heat of the moment. For a minute, it looked like one of those prison riots. Quentin had to be taken to the nurse's office, and Mummy had to come to school to take him home.

Later that day, Claudine and Bessie were told to stop by Miss Trisket's office after school. They found Forbush there with Trisket. Forbush pointed a finger at Bessie.

"You're the pencil girl!"

"Yes, ma'am."

A grin they'd never seen before brightened Forbush's face.

"I've told that story fifty times since then! And you're the brains of the gang of two, Claudine?—no offense, Bessie! Now listen! No one must ever know anything about this but us four."

"Our lips are sealed!"

"They'd better be, or they'll never taste my pizza again!"

"I hope we're having it tomorrow!"

"No, tomorrow's from the cookbook again. Vegetable Mixer."

"Have to rub it in a little more, just to make the point," said Trisket.

"But by Wednesday, we'll be back on course," promised Forbush.

Claudine cackled.

"Mrs. Willoughby's not going to like this," she predicted.

Whereupon Forbush bristled.

"Well, if she doesn't like it, she can—"

"Now, now!" Trisket held up her hands, and grinned at the girls. "You see what I mean about great cooks? They're temperamental!"

Sad to say, Gwendolyn Willoughby was absent once more the day after Broccoli Surprise.

She'd broken out in spots again!

SIX

• • • • • • • • • •

Redfang was on the warpath again. This time it was Cleanup Week.

Having noted with horror various candy bar wrappers, apple cores, Popsicle sticks, orange peel, chocolate milk cartons, and other flotsam and jetsam and generally ugly litter in the grass and shrubbery and on the playground, he had ordered the entire student body to get down on its hands and knees and clean up the mess. Each class was assigned a different section of the grounds at various times during the week.

In general, he was grudgingly satisfied with the results. Only the third grade disgraced itself. The third grade was assigned the shrubbery on the north side of the building. The principal's office was on that side.

"This afternoon, after the third grade had supposedly completed its task, I happened to glance out my window, and what did I see on the ground directly under it? A beer can!"

As a result, the third grade was scheduled to be sent out the next day fifteen minutes before the end of classes to crawl into the north shrubbery again and DO THEIR JOB PROPERLY. Claudine gave Ferdy a pep talk that morning while they were waiting for Mr. Feeney's schoolbus to show up.

"Listen, get those creeps of yours going this time, Ferdy, or he'll be on all our backs! How you dummies could miss a *beer can* beats me, anyway. Don't you have any pride in your school?"

"No."

Of course, he didn't really mean that, but it was fun to talk that way. Claudine gave up.

"Got your baseball?"

"Sure! It's in my backpack. I'm going to show it to everybody!"

As usual, Ferdy was wearing one of his favorite possessions—a canvas backpack. He carried everything he took to school in it.

"With that thing on," Claudine decided, "you look like a hunchbacked gnome."

Ferdy didn't even bother to hit her. He knew exactly what he really looked like—a fearless mountain climber—because when he had first put it on, he had admired himself in the mirror several times.

On the way to school, Ferdy showed his prize

baseball to everybody on the bus. Sitting with Bessie, Claudine explained.

"You know what a big Red Sox fan Ferdy is, and Hank Foley is his idol," she said, mentioning a Boston superstar. "Well, Uncle Larry went to a game last week in Chicago and who should hit a foul ball that Uncle Larry caught but Hank Foley? So Uncle Larry got Foley to autograph it, and sent it to Ferdy. Talk about excited! We had to grab his ankles to keep him from floating away!"

The school day passed without incident. On their way out to the bus, Claudine said, "Let's go around and see how Ferdy's doing in the bushes, Bessie. Look, there goes Redfang."

Mr. Kleinstein was bustling away in the direction of the parking lot, probably on his way to some meeting.

"I guess he's been out there supervising things," said Bessie.

"Sure. I'm surprised he's not carrying his bullhorn."

The third graders were straggling out of the shrubbery with small plastic litter bags. They emptied the bags into the large bag their teacher, Mr. Randall, was holding, while he chatted with Miss Finch and Mrs. Hindle. Claudine looked around for Ferdy.

"Where is that squirt?" she wondered as they strolled past the bushes. "Hey, Ferdy, what are you doing? Time to go!"

"In here!" called Ferdy. "Come look!"

"What now?"

"Hurry!"

Claudine rolled her eyes, put down her books, and ducked under a tangle of shrubbery. Ferdy was on his hands and knees, staring at a green object on a twig.

"Look! The biggest praying mantis I ever saw, eating a fly!" he said with great satisfaction. Insects were one of his many hobbies.

"Yuk! You dragged me in here to watch a messy eater chew up a fat fly?"

"Flies are very nutritious!"

"Well, you can have my share. Come on, we've got to get going. You know Mr. Feeney. Where's your litter bag? Did you find anything interesting?"

"Naw, not even a beer can."

"Where's your backpack?"

"I took it off, it kept catching on things. It's right behind me."

Claudine peered around.

"It's not behind you anymore, it's way back under another bush."

"Well, I was stalking that praying mantis—"

"Never mind, go get it and let's move, or we'll be late for the bus. You're the last one in here!"

When they crawled out, Bessie asked, "What was it?"

"Nature study," said Claudine disgustedly. Ferdy pulled on his backpack and ran after them as they headed for the bus.

At home they dropped their stuff on the sofa and went straight to the neighborhood park—Ferdy to play baseball, and Claudine and Bessie to play tennis, if they could get on a court with some friends. Naturally Ferdy didn't even consider taking Foley to the park. Too many goony big kids around.

After supper they both went outside again for a while. When they came in, their mother pointed a stern finger at the sofa.

"I wish you two would stop using that as the town dump. When you come home, take your things to your room. I don't want to see anything on that sofa, etc., etc."—the lecture went on for a while. When it was over, Mr. Boggs looked up from his newspaper.

"Well, Ferdy, I'm glad your baseball was such a big hit at school. It was a bigger hit than *Foley's* been getting lately—he went 0 for 5 yesterday."

He was always making painful jokes like that.

"Aw, he's in a slump. It won't last," said Ferdy, and then his face brightened. "Listen, Mr. Randall said he'd show me how to make a stand for my baseball to sit on!"

Ferdy lifted the flap of his backpack and reached in for his prize possession. His face froze. He threw the flap back and scrabbled around frantically inside.

"It's gone! My baseball's gone!"

Given a shock like that, lots of third graders would have burst into tears. Ferdy, for one. He let out a howl that could have been heard over at Bessie's house. Everybody gathered around.

"I told you over and over to fasten those flap straps, but oh, no, you couldn't be bothered!" said Claudine, by way of offering comfort. Oddly enough, her kind words didn't seem to help one bit.

"*How* could it fall out?" he yelled bitterly—and abruptly stopped crying. "Wait a minute! I know! It's that darn old Redfang and his darn old Cleanup Week! It must have fallen out when I was crawling around under those darn old bushes, before I took it off. That's *gotta* be it! Come on, we gotta go look for it right away!"

"Now, wait a minute. Take it easy, son," said Mr. Boggs, as Ferdy charged toward the door. "You're probably right—I'm sure you're right—but nobody's going to be looking around in those bushes after dark, so it's perfectly safe till morning."

"What?" Ferdy was astounded by such parental stupidity. "Some buses get there before ours! Some other kid might see it and—"

Everybody got into the discussion, mostly in loud tones, but in the end Mrs. Boggs held up her hands, looked at her husband, and sighed.

"Listen, George, we might as well go. He won't sleep a wink tonight if we don't."

"Oh, for— The police are really out these days, keeping an eye on school grounds. If we go over there and start poking around in the bushes with flashlights . . ."

It didn't do him any good. In the end, they all piled in the car and went.

They put the car in the parking lot and walked self-consciously across the dark, empty, silent school grounds toward the dark, empty, silent school.

"All right, now," snapped Father Boggs. "Where were you?"

Ferdy marched toward the bushes, took a measuring look this way and that, and stuck his hand out in front of him.

"Right . . . here!"

"Good!"

"I think," he added.

"Oh, for— Can't you remember exactly? Claudine, you went in there with him, can't you remember?"

"It was right about in here somewhere," said Claudine none too exactly herself. "We'll have to look around a little."

"Well, get in there and make it snappy!" said their father, shooting a hunted look over his shoulder. "Here, give me a flashlight, I'll go, too!"

Of course, in no time at all they heard gruff voices saying, "What's going on here?" and Mrs. Boggs saying, "Why—er—we're looking for a baseball we lost," and a gruff voice saying, "Come on, lady, you gonna tell us you were playing catch in the pitch dark?"

At that point, Mr. Boggs poked his head out of the bushes and squinted in the glare of the official flashlight that was turned on him. As he snarled later, "A grown man on his hands and knees in the bushes at night? *Of course* I felt silly!" Claudine and

Ferdy climbed out behind him, at which point Mrs. Boggs swept a hand at her family.

"Listen, do we look like the Mafia?"

The policemen began to grin.

"Well, no."

"Our idiot son here managed to lose a special baseball, and he thinks he lost it here," said Mr. Boggs. "It's got Hank Foley's autograph on it."

"Hank Foley? Well, that's different!"

But even with two police officers lending their expert help, they could not find Ferdy's baseball.

SEVEN

• • • • • • • • • • • • •

When they got home, they sat down around the kitchen table and had milk or coffee, according to ages, while Mr. Boggs played detective.

"Now, let's assume the ball didn't fall out of Ferdy's backpack, because if it had we should have found it. So if it didn't fall out, then someone *took* it out. How far from the bag had Ferdy crawled, Claudine?"

"Well . . . at least ten feet, maybe more."

"And Ferdy was watching a praying mantis, and we all know what he's like when he's watching an insect."

"Anyone could have taken anything out of that bag and Ferdy wouldn't have heard him," said Mrs. Boggs.

"And every kid in the third grade knew he'd

brought the ball with him, so any one of them might have taken it," said Mr. Boggs. "The problem now is to eliminate some of them and narrow it down—"

"Rottenquentin!" cried Claudine and Ferdy in the same breath.

"Well! That's what I call pretty fast narrowing down. Okay, let's assume it was Quentin, if only because he makes such a perfect suspect. Even if he took it, would he dare put it in his own bag and—"

"That wimp carries a satchel," said Ferdy, "a fancy leather satchel with his initials on it—"

"So if he took the ball and put it in his satchel, how could he be sure Ferdy wouldn't look in his backpack two minutes later and see the ball was missing? And then maybe everyone would be lined up and—"

"He wouldn't take a chance like that," agreed Claudine. "He's a sly one."

"So if he took the ball, and didn't dare come out of the bushes with it, what would he do?"

"Hide it somewhere!" cried Ferdy. "That would be just like him! And his bus gets to school before ours does, so he can grab my baseball in the morning before we get there!"

"Please remember that it *could* be someone besides Rotten—besides Quentin," said Mr. Boggs, sounding for the present like the schoolteacher that, after all, he was. "But if someone *did* hide it, and someone *does* take it again in the morning, then you'll have a chance to get it back. But you mustn't just go to school tomorrow morning and start accusing any-body—"

"Not even Rottenquentin?"

"Not even Rotten, as you say, Quentin. You must tell Mr. Randall about all this, and let him handle it. I'm sure he'll be able to arrange a discreet way of checking around and seeing if your ball is in anyone's possession."

Claudine looked doubtful. She shook her head and spoke in dark tones.

"I don't know. Like I said, he's a sly one!"

"Now, listen, fun's fun, but you two have got to stop this!" said Mr. Boggs. "Quentin Willoughby may have his faults, but the chances that he had any-thing to do with this are very slim. Think of what the odds are! He'd have had to be crawling around in those bushes in just the right place at just the right time—"

"He's just the one who could do it," said Clau-dine, and got a lecture on Being Fair to People We Don't Like.

The next morning, Ferdy could hardly wait to get going on criminal detection. Overnight he had transformed himself into Sherlock Holmes, Jr. Clau-dine had been doing a lot of thinking, too. It came as quite a shock to both of them, however, to arrive at school and be sent straight to the principal's office.

"What does he want us for?" Claudine wondered uneasily, but Ferdy, though trembling, was an opti-mist.

"Maybe someone found my ball!"

"Are you kidding? Do you think he'd bother with that? And anyway—why me, too?"

Claudine knew from experience that in her case no good was likely to come from a summons to the Lion's Den. And of course she was right. When they entered the lair and stood in front of his desk, the King of the Beasts looked ready to spring. He turned his fiery gaze on quivering Ferdy, and suddenly his right hand thrust the baseball at him, Foley autograph forward.

"Ferdinand, is this yours?"

Ferdinand's eyes looked about the same size as the baseball.

"Gee! Yes, sir, that's it!"

"Then how does it happen I found it in my office when I came in this morning? I had left my window open. Mr. Franzen closed it later in the afternoon, and didn't notice that anything was amiss," said Mr. Kleinstein in an aggrieved tone of voice. Mr. Franzen was the head custodian, and Mr. Franzen rarely noticed anything.

"Obviously this baseball was tossed into my office sometime during the third grade's shrubbery cleanup—*second* shrubbery cleanup, I might add—and it bounced onto my desk and knocked one of the pens out of my desk set! I'm surprised it wasn't broken! Now, how did *your* baseball get in here, that's what I want to know!"

Ferdy and Claudine exchanged a wide-eyed look of genuine amazement, and even under the stress and strain of the moment Claudine had a hard time not grinning. Everybody in school knew about that desk set, that black marble stand with two pens in brass holders and places for pencils and paper clips, and a little brass plate on the front of it that said:

PRESENTED TO

RONALD J. KLEINSTEIN

ELEMENTARY SCHOOL PRINCIPAL OF THE YEAR

BY

MAYOR CYRUS WADKINS

and gave the date, which was two years ago. It was Mr. Kleinstein's pride and joy.

But, as Redfang had asked, how had the ball gotten in there? It was an interesting question.

"G-gosh, Mr. Kleinstein, I don't know!" stammered Ferdy.

The fiery gaze swiveled in Claudine's direction.

"Well, I can tell you this—not only was Ferdinand the last third grader to leave the bushes yesterday afternoon, but he called to you, Claudine, and you were observed crawling into the bushes to join him. One teacher felt it her duty to report these facts when she heard about the incident this morning."

Miss Finch, of course. She was a great one for feeling her duty. Now Claudine was aroused.

"But, Mr. Kleinstein, that's Ferdy's special baseball—"

"I know all about that. Mr. Randall told me."

"Well, Ferdy was about as likely to throw that baseball in here as—as you would be to throw your desk set out! Somebody else snuck it out of his bag and threw it!"

Mr. Kleinstein leaned back and put his fingers together carefully into a steeple. He nodded.

"That seems quite likely. But at the same time, Ferdinand *could* be talked into an audacious prank if he thought there would be no danger of his not getting his ball back simply because it seemed so completely improbable that he would ever do such a thing. Much as it pains me to rake up the past, Claudine, I cannot help but feel this sort of prank has a familiar ring to it—a terribly familiar ring. I cannot help recalling a couple of incidents when *you* were in the third grade, not to mention a few others since then. . . .

"Well, I'll tell you what I'm going to do." He leaned forward and positioned the baseball with fussy precision in front of the desk set. "I'm going to allow time for the culprit to come forward in a manly—or womanly—way and admit to this incident, at which time I shall have a few words to say to him or her, but will take no further action. Forgive and forget shall be my motto in this instance. But until that time, the baseball shall remain right here. Now, you may return to your classes and think it over. And if someone else does come forward, I shall be the first to apologize to you both."

As they went off down the hall together, Claudine fumed under her breath.

"It isn't fair! We didn't do it, and he shouldn't keep your ball!"

"He *will* give it back, won't he?" asked Ferdy anxiously.

"Oh, sure—at the end of the school year! It's not fair!"

"Who ever said he was fair?"

"Well, he usually is, in a sort of way. . . . But this time . . ."

The word went around that whoever had thrown Ferdy's ball into Mr. Kleinstein's office would get a lecture but no punishment if he or she came forward, but no one did. Day after day, Ferdy's ball sat there on Mr. Kleinstein's desk, in front of the desk set, facing the door, and every time the door was open when she walked past and could see the ball, Claudine grew more annoyed.

"Well, anyway, that was some fancy shot, to hit the desk and knock over a pen," said Bessie. "Whoever did it ought to take up bowling."

"My money's still on Rottenquentin!"

"You'll never be able to nail him."

"I suppose not. But it isn't fair!"

Then one morning they were making second copies of one-page essays they had written—Mrs. Hindle was the old-fashioned kind of teacher who actually made them learn how to write things. Hunched over her desk, Claudine was turning out her usual scratchy mess. She glanced enviously at Bessie's paper. Bessie had the best handwriting in the class. Claudine sighed, and then suddenly blinked, and thought for a moment. Then she sighed again.

"Not a chance," she said to herself. But even so, she decided that from now on, she would come prepared, just in case.

It was recess time two days later, and a beautiful morning, so everybody else rushed outside while Claudine waited for Bessie to pick up some papers she had dropped. As they passed the school office, she heard Mr. Kleinstein's secretary, Mrs. Harper, telling someone on the phone that he had gone to a meeting. And when they were passing his private office, Claudine decided he must have been in a hurry, because his door had been left open. Not only was his door open, not one soul was around anywhere.

Claudine didn't quite get past.

Bessie gasped.

"Claudine! What are you doing?"

As she always could when she wanted to, chunky Claudine moved like lightning. She was back almost instantly, and she had the baseball.

"Come on! We've got just enough time! It's a piece of cake!" she said, and hurried Bessie back down the hall to their empty classroom. She rushed to her desk, stuck her hand deep into her schoolbag, and brought out another baseball.

"This is one of Ferdy's regular ones, a new one he hasn't even used yet." She held the two balls side by side. "See? You can't tell 'em apart, except for Foley's autograph. Now, get busy and copy that onto this ball!"

"What?"

Bessie's voice sounded shrill and incredulous—but at the same time she was reaching for her pen.

"Black. Be sure it's black."

"It is." Bessie giggled hysterically, and went to work. The result might not have been an exact copy, but you would have needed to look at both baseballs to tell the difference.

"Great!" Claudine tucked the Foley ball away in her bag. "Now let's get this one on his desk and we're all set!"

"Claudine, you are the limit!"

"Come on, and be quiet!"

Claudine was almost out the door when a dreadful sound stopped her in her tracks and turned her to stone.

"Mrs. Harper!"

"Yes, Mr. Kleinstein?"

"Mrs. Harper, the baseball is gone! Someone has taken that baseball!"

Claudine turned a pale face back at Bessie.

"My gosh, he's back already!"

Simba's roar continued to fill the hallways.

"Well, I know one thing—I want to see a certain young lady and I want to see her now!"

"Yes sir! You mean—"

The voices receded, along with Mr. Kleinstein's heavy footsteps and the click of Mrs. Harper's high heels. Claudine peeped out. They were just disappearing out the front doors. Claudine breathed again.

"Come on! Quick!"

They rushed down the hall to the den and then

straight to Trisket's office, where they burst in and threw themselves on her mercy.

"Save us!"

Trisket leaned back from her desk.

"Oh, good grief—what now?"

They told her all. Once again she had to resort to her box of tissues.

"Well, I must say, you do brighten a day. Okay, what's your plan, Claudine?"

By this time, the King of the Beasts was returning to his lair, and he was licking his lips as though anticipating a very satisfying meal.

"There's your answer!" he was saying to Mrs. Harper as they came down the hall. "Claudine Boggs is not outside anywhere, but she is present *somewhere.* I want her found and brought to my office!" he was saying as he turned to enter it.

He stopped short. He stared. He roared.

"Mrs. Harper!"

"Y-yes, sir?"

"Now my *desk set* is gone, too!"

Before he could have an apoplectic fit, however, Mrs. Harper scurried into his office, took a frantic look around, and cried in a vastly relieved tone of voice, "Oh, Mr. Kleinstein, here they are on your bookcase—the desk set *and* the ball!"

At that moment, a pathetic little procession came up the hall from the direction of Miss Trisket's office. Bessie Emanuelson was tottering along, held by Trisket on one side and Claudine Boggs on the other.

64

"Now, Bessie," Nurse Trisket was saying, "if you have any more dizziness at all, I want Claudine to bring you back to my office right away and you're going to lie down until— Oh, hello, Mr. Kleinstein! Poor Bessie had another of her dizzy spells, I'm afraid, but we hope she's all right now."

Bessie let out a strange sound. It was as though, by a tremendous effort, she had managed to turn a giggle into a pitiful whimper. Mr. Kleinstein made some strange sounds, too. He seemed to be momentarily incapable of speech. They turned the corner and helped poor Bessie on down the hall to Mrs. Hindle's classroom.

Mrs. Harper crept out into the hall. Mr. Kleinstein stood there grinding his teeth, clenching his fists, and with his face inventing a new shade of purple.

"Mrs. Harper, I don't trust . . . I don't trust—*anybody!*" he snarled, and stamped into his office, slamming the door behind him so hard the baseball rolled off onto the floor.

EIGHT

••••••••••••

For a week, Gwendolyn Willoughby had been walking around wearing a smug look that, as Bessie said, "made you want to smack it off her face!" She had also been dropping mysterious hints to her friends in the presence of her enemies.

"I'm going to have a very special birthday this year—just you wait and see!"

Or,

"This time it's not going to be just any old party—but I can't say anything about it quite yet!"

As Claudine said to Bessie, "If that isn't saying anything about it, I don't know what saying anything about it is."

"What's 'it'?" wondered Bessie. "What's she up to now?"

"I don't know, but she's got all the wimps' tongues hanging out."

Then one morning Gwen breezed into school, glowing with self-importance, and released the big news.

"Mummy and Daddy are giving me an extraspecial birthday party this year—at the Country Club! Oh, I'm so glad my birthday's on a Friday, because there'll be music and dancing and everything!"

"Just your family?" asked someone.

"You gonna take a date?" asked someone else.

Gwendolyn looked down her nose at one and all and made use of her silvery laugh.

"Don't be silly! I'm having whoever I want—and I won't just go around *asking* kids, like for an *ordinary* birthday party. We're *mailing* out the invitations!"

For the next day or two, Gwendolyn basked in the limelight, keeping even her friends on tenterhooks, refusing to talk about whom she was going to invite. Claudine was disgusted.

"Can't you see them rushing home every day— 'Mom! Mom! Did the mailman bring me anything?' "

"Well, we all know *one* who'll get invited and be her date, anyway," said Bessie. "Roddy Plover."

Roddy Plover's family was the most prominent and richest family in town, even richer than Gwen's. Roddy took himself very seriously, and although he was not the stupidest kid in class, he certainly managed to be the stuffiest.

"You won't get an argument from me," agreed Claudine. "Her whole family's always sucking up to the Plovers."

Then one morning, the smug looks in their class increased tenfold—worn by the ten kids who received invitations to the big party.

"Not a surprise in the lot," said Claudine, once the returns were in. "Wall-to-wall wimps."

They were standing in the hall talking, she and Bessie, when Maureen Beesley, another reject, joined them just as Gwen went past with one of her worshipers, Boo Middleton. Gwen's glance darted sideways, and she lifted the decibel level of her conversation.

"Of course, I wish I could invite just *everybody,* but you can't do it, even at a big place like the Country Club, especially not when you think what it's going to cost Mummy and Daddy!"

"Hey, Boo, I didn't know you were getting deaf!" yelled Claudine.

"Aw, shut up, Claudine!" snapped Boo, who didn't have much of an arsenal of snappy repartee. Gwendolyn attempted to annihilate Claudine with a single scornful glance.

"I wasn't talking to you, Fatso!"

"Why don't you borrow Simba's bullhorn?" asked Claudine.

Gwendolyn was furious, because she had felt she was being subtle and clever.

"Oh, come on, Boo. We're wasting our time!" They marched off down the hall.

"Aw, who wants to go to her old party, anyway?" whined Maureen. Claudine glanced at her and sighed. Maureen Beesley was a wimp who didn't even make it as a wimp.

The next day Claudine and Bessie were passing Trisket's office when they heard sounds of great hilarity within. Lots of girlish laughter, no doubt about it. They stopped and looked at each other.

"What's that all about?" wondered Bessie.

"Sounds like Trisket and Forbush to me."

"Yep. Nice they got to be such pals."

The door opened. Forbush started to come out, then looked at them with surprise.

"Well, speaking of the Devil!"

"Who?"

"You!" she said, pointing at them both. "We were just talking about you."

Trisket peered around the corner from behind her desk.

"Hey, come in a minute, girls," she said. "You won't believe this!"

Forbush shut the door behind them.

"I was just telling Miss Forbush about what you did to Kenneth Barr," said Trisket.

Claudine's eyes widened.

"Everything?"

"Everything," said Forbush, and laid a hand on each of their heads. "Bless you both. He deserved that and worse, the rat!"

Bessie goggled at Forbush through her glasses.

"Gosh! You mean, you were another of his—his—"

"Victims?" said Claudine, to avoid whatever word Bessie might be coming up with.

"Certainly not!" Forbush bridled at the very idea. "I wouldn't have dated that pompous idiot if—if— It was much worse than that. I only saw him once—briefly—and that was enough. I don't even want to talk about it!"

"Oh, please, tell us what happened!"

"I'll die if you don't!" promised Bessie.

Forbush simmered down, looked at them, and smiled. Actually, she was very pretty when she smiled.

"Okay, I guess I owe you one. Well, what happened was, last year I was working my way through my final year at Cornell by being the salad chef in the local restaurant—and you can imagine how hard it was to get a job like that in a place where so many were training to work in the business.

"Well, one night everything went wrong at the restaurant, the boss was jumping on everyone, and we were all on edge. For one thing, we had a big party coming in from the school, a bunch from the English department entertaining a visiting author of children's books—they had a seminar for people interested in writing children's books. So pretty soon, the boss came back and said, 'Now, we got this famous author I never heard of coming tonight, and I want everything to be just right!' Well, they had their soup and that was fine, and meantime they'd ordered what kind of salad dressing they wanted. I was getting the salads ready, but we all managed to take a peek out the kitchen doors to see what this famous author looked like. And here was this real handsome character right out of the movies. And one of the waitresses got so excited she turned around and dumped over the whole bowl of my best lettuce onto the kitchen floor.

"Well, you can imagine what we went through, picking up that lettuce and washing it off, all the time with one eye over our shoulders watching for a health inspector. Well, somehow I got everything together, and we were only a little late sending the salads in to the table—and of course with the boss on our necks, chewing us out every minute. By the time the waitresses took them in, I was a wreck. I had to sit down for a minute. But I'd hardly sat down when one of the girls came back looking like the end of the earth.

" '*He* wants to see you,' she said.

" 'Who? The boss?' I said.

" 'No. That author. He asked for the salad chef.'

"Well, from the way she looked, I didn't figure he was going to tell me how great my salad was, so I guess when I got up and walked out there I already had a chip on my shoulder. But then! You know what he did? He looked up at me in this superior way, and said he'd ordered the house dressing, hoping for the best, but it was really inedible. Then he started to explain to me how you should go about making a good salad dressing.

"Well, he didn't get very far. You know what I did? I said, 'Oh, you don't like it this way, sir? Well, then, try it *this* way!' And I picked up his salad bowl and dumped his whole salad right on his head!"

Claudine and Bessie had to hold onto each other, otherwise they would have been rolling on the floor.

"Oh, that's the best thing I ever heard!" cried Bessie.

"Poor old Dingle!" giggled Claudine.

"Poor old Dingle my eye!" snapped Forbush. "It may sound funny now, but I can tell you it wasn't then. That was the end of my job at the Campus Café, and I had a terrible time before I got a job anywhere else! So of all the people in the world, Mr. Dingle-Barr is the one I despise the most!"

NINE

· · · · · · · · · · ·

"What a story!" said Claudine. She looked as gratified as if she'd just finished a hot fudge sundae. "I'm only sorry you weren't here when he came to talk to us. If you'd *both* been here, he *really* would have flipped!"

"He wouldn't know me from Adam," said Forbush. "Like I said, we met *very* briefly."

"You could have reminded him."

Suddenly Trisket remembered what time it was.

"Say, what are you two doing here this late? The buses left ages ago."

"We've got a couple of things to do on the way; we're going to walk home. So we took our time."

"Anyway, tomorrow's pizza day—we've got to work up our appetites," said Bessie.

"Not me," said Claudine. "I always wish I could have one more piece—of course, I know you can't let us have more than one or you'd never get finished."

Trisket and Forbush exchanged a glance.

"What do you think, Inga?"

"Sure, why not?"

Trisket turned to Claudine and Bessie.

"Tomorrow after school Miss Forbush is going to show me how to make a pizza—"

"I always have some leftover dough—"

"And if you girls would like to come and watch, too—"

"Wow! Great!"

"But don't tell anybody else, because we don't want a crowd. And I'll drop you off at home afterwards."

The girls left the building glorying in their good luck.

"What a treat, Claudine!"

"Yes—and if she bakes a pizza, somebody's going to have to help eat it!"

They were still chattering away happily when they left the school grounds and walked down Prairie Avenue. Up ahead of them, a man got out of a car parked at the curb. He had a dark mustache and a beard flecked with gray, and hair about the same color, and he was wearing round glasses that made him look very solemn. So did his black suit. As he came around the front of his car to the sidewalk, he seemed to walk with a slight limp.

"Pardon me, young ladies," he said in a voice with just a hint of a foreign accent about it, "do you attend this school—Gruberville Elementary School, I believe it is?"

They stopped and Claudine said, "Yes, sir. Why?"

"Could you tell me, do you have a dietitian at your school?"

"Sure!"

"And could you tell me her name?"

"Inga Forbush."

The strange foreigner seemed to quiver at the mention of her name, but he quickly said, "Ah, yes, Forbush. That's the one. And Inga, eh? A Scandinavian name, a variation of Ingrid. Perhaps she is part Swedish, as I am."

"Are you? Gee, I'm *all* Swedish!" said Bessie.

"We can't all be so lucky," said the stranger. "Well, now, as it happens, I am also a chef, a great chef—in my native country, one of the most renowned. I wonder if you might know my name?"

"Well, I doubt it, we don't know much about great chefs," said Claudine politely, "but—what is it?"

The man leaned forward and stuck his face right in hers.

"My name," he said, "is Harold Dingle! How are you, Claudine? Hi, Bessie! How do you like my disguise? It never fails! Come on, get in the car—I want to talk to you!"

"If the police stop me for picking up schoolgirls," he said as they drove off, "remember to tell them I'm your uncle. Now, look here—when I saw you coming I realized I'd been missing a bet. Your scheming mind is just what I need, Claudine. And after what you put me through—which worked out very well, I'll admit—I consider you both old friends. And what are old friends for if not to help each other?"

"Mr. Barr—"

"Never mind the formalities, if we're going to work together call me Kenny. I hate Harold."

"Okay, Kenny, but what—"

"I've come back here to Gruberville for just one purpose."

"What's that?"

Kenny Barr groaned.

"To exorcise Inga Forbush out of my life! That girl has possessed me long enough!"

"Possessed you?" cried Bessie, excited now. "You mean, you roll around in bed talking in a funny voice and saying dirty words?"

He chuckled bitterly.

"No, not that bad—but bad enough! When I was here—when was it?—a couple of months ago—I was having one of my free intervals. I thought I'd finally shaken her off. But she's back! Oh, yes, she's back, and worse than ever! So I checked with Cornell and found out she's here!"

"Gosh, this is funny!" said Bessie. "She was just—ow!"

Claudine's elbow had given her a sharp message.

"Oh, excuse me, Bessie. She was in the hall just now when we came out," said Claudine, finishing Bessie's remark for her. "But how come you know *her,* too? Her and Trisket both! Golly, do you know every pretty lady in every school in the country?"

"Not quite. I think there are three in Utah I've missed. And I don't really *know* that Forbush shrew at all, I haven't even met her—it was more of an encounter. Under the worst possible circumstances."

"What happened? I mean, if we're going to help you do whatever it is you want to do, we need to know—"

Kenny Barr turned the car into one of their favorite places, one Claudine had not been allowed to see much of lately—Gino's Ice Cream Drive-In.

"We'd better have something to keep us going," he said. "You just won't believe what you're about to hear."

He didn't get any argument from his passengers. When they had ordered, he sat back from the steering wheel and began.

"This goes back about a year. Have you ever heard of Cornell University?"

"Sure! Forbush went there."

"She sure did! And she as working in a place called the Campus Café when I came to Cornell to do a workshop with some of their English majors. They took me to dinner at the café, which they said was the best place around. Well, the soup was all right—I would have used less curry, but no matter—and then on came the salad. I had ordered the house dressing, hoping against hope it would be palatable, but when it came, it wasn't. It had a funny taste. Now, I happen to be an outstanding cook myself—that's why I use a 'great chef' character for my disguise, because I can always live up to it—and one of my strongest points is salads and salad dressings. I asked who their salad chef was. They said a senior from the Cornell cooking school. So I thought the nice thing to do would be to give the kid some tips on how to make a really superb salad dressing, like the ones I make myself."

Bessie uttered a strange gurgling sound at that point, causing Claudine to hit her smartly on the back.

"What's the matter with you, Bessie?"

"I think I swallowed a gnat," she said, choking. "I'll be all right."

Fortunately their hot fudge sundaes arrived, which gave Bessie a chance to get a grip on herself before Kenny went on.

"So I told the waitress I'd like to see the salad chef. She went and got her. In came this tall blonde with hard eyes—I should have known right away she was trouble, but I didn't really take her in till too late. I told her in the nicest possible way that her salad dressing just wouldn't do, and then I began to explain how it should be made. But I'd hardly begun when that she-devil started yelling at me. 'You don't like it my way, huh?' she said. 'Well, then, try it *this* way!' she said, and she picked up my salad bowl and dumped the whole greasy mess all over my head and my three-hundred-dollar suit!"

Kenny paused and stared at them, to let this blockbuster sink in.

"I've had that suit cleaned four times since then, but it's never come out quite right."

"You've got some hot fudge on your beard," Claudine told him, and while he was tidying it up, she went on. "Well, that sounds like a terrible experience, but if she did that to you, why do you want to see her again?"

"Are you planning some horrible revenge?" asked Bessie breathlessly.

Kenny Barr sighed deeply. His eyes brooded into space behind the round spectacles.

"No. Rotten as she was to me, I want no revenge. I just want to be free of her!"

"What do you mean?"

He turned his head to look at them, and he was so shaken that his plastic ice-cream paddle rattled in his plastic cup.

"Would you believe it, I can't get her out of my mind! I never saw anyone look as beautiful when she was mad as she did!"

"She's pretty when she smiles, too," said Claudine.

"I wouldn't know," grumped Kenny, "I've never seen her smile. Well, anyway. At first, I thought I'd soon forget all about her, but then I couldn't get her off my mind. I'd wake up in the middle of the night seeing her as she stood back with that empty salad bowl in her hands—blazing with beauty! Magnificent! Sometimes she'd go away for a couple of weeks, but then suddenly she'd be back. So finally I decided I'd have to do something about it. What I want is a chance to see her face to face, without her knowing it's me, so that I can get her out of my mind. I *know* she can't be as sensational as I remember her, I'm *sure* if I could just spend a few minutes with her she'd turn out to be nothing outstanding—a fairly ordinary girl—oh, good-looking in an average way, but I've known hundreds of girls I'm sure were better-looking than that witch!"

Claudine already had a dreamy, faraway look on her face.

"Tomorrow," she said. "Tomorrow after school she's going to show Trisket how to make a pizza, and they said we could come, too."

"Pizza! Well, if there's anything I know—"

"And Bessie is Swedish, so you could be her Swedish uncle who's visiting her family and is a great chef. We can tell Forbush we've told you what a good cook she is, so if we ask her if you can come, too, I'm sure she'll say it's okay. . . ."

For a moment, Kenny Barr stared at Claudine with awe. Then he smiled delightedly.

"Claudine, you've got a great criminal mind! The minute I saw you coming, I knew I could count on you. Okay, now, let's work out the details!"

TEN

· · · · · · · · · ·

When the great Swedish chef showed up the next afternoon, the girls let him in the back doors, the same way he had entered the first time he visited the school. As Claudine had explained ahead of time,

"Mr. Kleinstein may still be hanging around in his office, and he's always nosy about anyone he sees coming in after hours. We don't need him butting in today!"

Kenny's disguise was exactly the same as it had been the day before. His accent, if anything, was a little more Swedish.

"Now, don't forget, I'm Mr. Thor Thorgeson," he reminded them, having briefed them the day before. "That's the name I always use."

"We told her already," said Claudine.

Being as quiet as possible, they hurried down the

hall, turned in through the cafeteria doors, and entered the kitchen, where Forbush and Trisket were waiting. Both smiled brightly at the nice-looking gentleman who came in behind the girls.

"This is my Uncle Thor—Mr. Thor Thorgeson," said Bessie. "This is Miss Trisket and Miss Forbush, Uncle Thor."

"It's very kind of you to let me join you today," he said, and Forbush smiled at him again. The first time she smiled, Uncle Thor had seemed to sway a little. The second time, he suddenly took his handkerchief out of his pocket and mopped his brow.

"My, it's warm in here, isn't it—but then I'm used to it," he added quickly. "We cooks have to learn to take the heat, don't we, Miss Forbush? Ah! I see you have begun to roll out your pizza dough! And you have your saucepan of tomato sauce ready to heat—and the cheese? What cheese are you using? Ah, mozzarella! Good, good!"

Uncle Thor's eyes had lighted up, and he moved toward the counter compulsively. With delicate fingers, he lifted the edge of the rolled-out pizza dough and pinched it ever so gently. His face fell ever so slightly.

"Oh, dear. Good, good, yet not quite . . . Now, if I may say so, I would use just a bit more water and probably a small extra pinch of—"

A tall blonde with hard eyes was suddenly staring at him.

"*You!*" she cried. "It's *you!*"

She gave the girls a single, scathing, I'll-tend-to-you-later glance, then picked up the pizza dough and brought it down over their visitor's head. When she had finished, he was wearing a pizza-dough collar, and she was reaching for the saucepan.

"No! Please! Not the tomato sauce!" cried Kenny, backing away, and he looked so miserable that Forbush stayed her hand. "I can't believe it! My disguise has never failed me!"

"It didn't now!" she assured him in ringing tones. "It was that voice, that pompous voice telling *me* how to make pizza dough, just like it told *me* how to make salad dressing! I've never forgotten the sound of that voice, it's stayed with me ever since!"

"It has?" All at once Kenny Barr brightened up. "You mean, you've never forgotten me, either?"

Miss Forbush was suddenly flustered.

"What do you mean, *either?*"

"I mean, ever since that night you dumped that greasy salad on my head—and I still say there was too much oil in the dressing, but never mind—ever since that night, I haven't been able to get you out of my head! The way you looked, like an angry goddess! And now I've seen you smile, and it's worse! I give up!"

"And just what is all this?"

They had been making quite a bit of noise, talking rather loudly, and in the excitement of the moment, nobody had noticed a new arrival. Simba had joined them on stealthy feet. He was staring around with incredulous eyes, seeing Miss Forbush and Miss Trisket and a gentleman with a foreign appearance who had a grotesque white collar of some sort around his neck—and Claudine and Bessie, which was all he needed to feel sure that some catastrophe was afoot.

Trisket blushed. Forbush paled. Bessie goggled. Claudine, for once, was tongue-tied. It was Kenny Barr who stepped into the breach.

"Mr. Kleinstein! This is not what it seems," he said. "And don't interrupt, because this is a serious matter!"

As he turned back to Forbush, he swept the round spectacles aside.

"Inga Forbush, will you—ow!" he said, as he ripped off his mustache, "will you marry me?"

Forbush gasped.

"What? Are you crazy?" she cried in a tone that was not entirely convincing. In a sort of desperate way, she tried to be haughty. "Inga Dingle? Do you think anybody would want to have a name like that?"

"Don't be silly! You'd be Inga Barr to practically everyone."

"My nickname's Candy," she said, and suddenly giggled helplessly.

"It is not! You're making that up! Good Lord!" Kenny Barr groaned again. "You're beautiful when you're mad, and you're gorgeous when you smile, but when you giggle—!"

He grabbed her, kissed her hard, and reeled back clutching his upper lip.

"Ow! That mustache was murder!"

Forbush was giggling again. Helplessly. Mr. Kleinstein was staring again, and looking stunned.

"Mr. Barr!"

Kenny Barr grabbed his hand and shook it heartily.

"Mr. Kleinstein, I'm glad you came! You're a father figure to us all! May I have the hand of your dietitian in marriage?"

"No!" Simba snatched his hand away looking horrified. "She's the best cook we've ever had!"

"Don't worry, Mr. Kleinstein, I'm not going *anywhere* in a hurry," said Forbush, and then quickly decided she should revise that statement. "I mean, I'm not going anywhere, period!"

But again, she didn't sound entirely convincing.

When, eventually, Simba tottered away back to his den, having decided there was nothing to be done about anything, and wishing he could figure out how Claudine Boggs fitted into things, the rest of them had a long talk. And when she had Heard All, Forbush declared severely,

"Claudine, you are a menace to society!"

"Why?" asked Claudine. "It all worked out fine, didn't it?"

"No!"

"It did, too!" said Kenny Barr. "Don't pay any

attention to her, Claudine, you were wonderful! If there's anything we could do for you, just say so, and—"

Claudine was dreaming again.

"Well," she murmured, "there is one thing. . . ."

It was Friday, and Gwendolyn was talking to an excited group of her friends in the hall. As Claudine and Bessie were passing by, Claudine stopped and said,

"Hey, Gwen, we're going to a party tonight, too!"

Gwendolyn sounded her silvery laugh.

"Are you? That's nice! What kind, a church social?"

"No, Trisket's boyfriend's family is having it for Forbush and *her* new boyfriend."

"Forbush? The pizza queen? She's finally got a boyfriend? Who is it, Mr. Franzen?"

"No, he's from out of town. But the funny thing is, we all know him!" said Claudine, and turned to leave.

"What do you mean, we all know him?" Gwen asked sharply. "Who is he?"

Claudine glanced back, and spoke over her shoulder.

"Kenneth Barr."

Gwen froze.

"Who?"

Claudine glanced back once more.

"Kenneth Barr!"

Gwen looked dangerously close to breaking out in spots again. She was frothing at the mouth.

"What? Kenneth Barr? He's going to be there? You're going to be with— You're lying! I don't believe it!"

"Okay, don't. Wait and read about it in the papers," said Claudine, and moved off majestically down the hall. As they went outside, with Gwendolyn Willoughby still yelling after them, Bessie cackled.

"When she's pushing Roddy Plover around the dance floor tonight, that'll give her something to think about!"

Claudine sighed.

"Poor Gwen. When we're eating pizza with our gang, and she's whooping it up with the wimps, I'll almost feel sorry for her."

"Don't," said Bessie. "I say, show 'em no mercy! I say, Down With Wimps!"